THE BASKET
COUNTS

To
Patrick

Here!" Mel Jensen shouted from the corner of the court.

Earl Stone glanced at him, then passed the ball quickly to Caskie Bennett running up behind him. Earl, or Stoney as the kids called him, screened for Caskie. Caskie shot. The ball arced toward the basket, hit the far side of the rim, and bounced off.

Mel fumed as he rushed in for the rebound. That was the second time he was in the clear and Stoney didn't pass to him.

Mel leaped. Several other pairs of arms stretched up, too. Dutch Fullmer, Quincy's tall center, reached higher than the others, pulled down the ball, whipped it out of Titan hands, then passed to a Quint in the corner. The Quint dribbled to the center line, passed to another Quint beelining toward the Titans' basket.

1

All five Titans rushed after him but he was too far in the lead. He leaped and laid the ball up against the boards. The big orange sphere wobbled through the net for two more points.

Mel glanced at the scoreboard. VISITORS — 6; HOME — 7. It could have been VISITORS — 4 and HOME — 9 if Stoney had thrown him the ball.

Mel looked at Coach Tom Thorpe sitting next to the other Hillcrest Titans. Didn't Coach see Stoney purposely ignoring him? Or didn't he care?

Mr. Corbin, Hillcrest's junior varsity coach, was refereeing this practice game between the Hillcrest Titans and the Quincy Quints. He handed the ball to Rick Longfoot, the Titans' right guard, gave a blast on his whistle, and the game resumed.

Rick tossed to Caskie. Caskie dribbled the ball up to the center line, crossed it, then bounced a pass to Skeet Robinson. Skeet feinted out a Quint guard, dribbled toward the keyhole, then stopped and took a quick look over his shoulder.

"Here!" shouted Mel as he ran up behind him.

Skeet passed to him and Mel dribbled to the corner. He started to take a set shot, but a Quint popped up in front of him. Mel pivoted so that his

2

back was to the guard and passed to Rick. Rick drove in, leaped. . . . A Quint leaped at the same time, pressed his hand on the ball, and the whistle shrilled.

"Jump ball!" yelled Mr. Corbin.

Rick tapped to Caskie. Caskie passed to Skeet, Skeet to Stoney. Mel ran down along the sideline, his right arm raised. He was in the clear. Stoney could pass him the ball if he wanted to. The nearest Quint to Mel was at least twenty feet away.

But again Stoney didn't pass to him. He passed to Caskie instead. Caskie stopped abruptly some ten feet from the basket and shot. The ball struck the far side of the ring, bounced high, then came down again, struck the front side of the ring, and bounced off toward the keyhole.

A flock of green uniforms, the Titans, and black-striped gold uniforms, the Quints, scrambled after the ball. A Titan got it. Mel Jensen.

He yanked the ball away from stubborn hands, drove in hard, laid it up. The ball arced, brushed against the boards, slipped through the net.

"Way to go, Mel!" yelled a high-pitched voice from the bench.

Mel grinned and waved to his buddy, Darryl Brady, sitting on the bench. He'd recognize Darryl's voice anywhere. Both Mel and Darryl were new in the Hillcrest School this year. Their families had moved this past summer into a section of Trexton where only one other black family lived. Mel's father was a dentist and Darryl's father was an electronics engineer.

Some neighbors had welcomed the new families warmly. Others had not.

"Don't worry," Dad had said after the first few days. "They'll get used to us and we'll get used to them. We sleep the same way, eat the same food, breathe the same air. They'll learn that nothing is different between us, black or white."

"It isn't *all* the whites, Dad," Mel said. "It's just a few."

He was thinking of Stoney and Caskie, although he knew there were others, too.

"I know," said Dad.

A horn sounded. Darryl and Pedro Dorigez ran onto the court. Darryl took Stoney's place, Pedro took Mel's.

The quarter soon ended and the game went into

the second period. Coach Thorpe put in Andy Head and Kim Nemeth, giving the whole team almost equal time on the court.

Resentment flashed through Mel when he saw that both Stoney and Caskie were ignoring Darryl, too. More than twice they could have passed the ball to Darryl. He had been in the clear, in a good spot to shoot. But they had ignored him, just as they had ignored Mel.

Darryl intercepted a pass from a Quint and dribbled the ball as hard as he could down the length of the court. Then he leaped, laid the ball up, and sank it for two points!

"All right!" yelled Darryl. "You don't have to pass it, Cas! I'll get that ball one way or another!"

That Darryl. He didn't care what he said or to whom he said it. Mel glanced at the coach. Coach Thorpe had cracked a grin. Mel was sure that there was very little that went unnoticed by the coach's alert eyes, and wondered if he would say anything to Caskie and Stoney about not passing to Mel and Darryl. Guess I'll just have to wait, Mel thought.

The game went through the third and fourth quarters with the two coaches putting in all their players and playing both man-to-man and zone defense. The Quints won by a narrow margin, 38–35. It's lucky, thought Mel, that it wasn't a league game.

The Titans and the Quints went to the locker rooms and showered. Mel was already under a shower, enjoying the cool, needlelike spray, when Darryl showed up and took another stall. Behind him came Caskie and the other members of the team.

"Nice game, Mel!" yelled Rick Longfoot.

"You, too, Rick!" said Mel with a laugh.

Stoney and Caskie looked at him and Darryl briefly as they went by to another shower stall. Neither said anything.

Mel was glad when he and Darryl were dressed and out of there. It was cold and wintry outside but more comfortable than being around Caskie Bennett and Stoney.

2

The next day was Thanksgiving. Mel thought he had never seen so much food on the table in his life. Right in the middle of it was a large, crisply cooked turkey. Mom and Dad sat at opposite ends of the table with Mel and Robby on one side and Cindy and their big sister Ruth on the other.

As was the Jensen tradition, each family member took a turn to say what he or she was thankful for. Everyone laughed when Cindy said she was thankful not to be sharing a bedroom with her big sister anymore. When it was his turn, Mel hesitated a bit. It didn't make sense to be thankful for the way Caskie and Stoney treated him.

But there were a lot of other things he was thankful for. Top of the list was having a place on the Titans.

All four children climbed into the bus Monday morning after the long Thanksgiving weekend. Cindy got off at the elementary school, Robby and Mel at the middle school, and Ruth, a sophomore, continued on to the high school.

Seeing Caskie and Stoney in his classes made Mel think of the ball game again. But it wasn't until the next day that thinking about them really bothered him. He wished he were like Darryl Brady. Hardly anything bothered Darryl. But Mel got to thinking so much about Caskie's and Stoney's treatment of him and Darryl at the last ball game that he couldn't think of geography in Ms. Agard's class at all.

Suddenly he realized that she was addressing him. "Melvin, I asked you a question. What is *quebracho* and what is made from it?"

Mel remembered that the class was studying the country of Argentina. He remembered reading about *quebracho*, but for the life of him he couldn't think of what it was and what was made from it.

"Did you study this chapter, Melvin?" Ms. Agard asked, peering directly at him through her blue-rimmed glasses.

"Yes, I did," he answered truthfully.

8

"Then why can't you answer the question?"

Mel shrugged. "I don't know." Quickly he took a stab at the answer. "It's a kind of mineral, isn't it?"

A burst of laughter broke from the class. "No, it isn't, Melvin." Ms. Agard glanced over his head. "Can you answer the question, Caskie?"

"It's a tree from which the people get tannin, stuff used . . . I mean a product used in tanning hides," answered Caskie.

"That's right," said Ms. Agard. "Do you remember that now, Melvin?"

Mel avoided her eyes. "Yes," he said, embarrassed.

It seemed hours before class was over. And all that time Ms. Agard didn't ask him another question. "What's the trouble, Melvin?" she asked quietly after the others had left the room. "You've always been prepared before. Why weren't you today?"

He shrugged again. "Just couldn't remember," he said.

"But you did study the chapter on Argentina?"

"Uh-huh. Yes."

Ms. Agard was quiet a moment. "You're on the basketball team, aren't you?"

"Yes."

"Has that got anything to do with it? Or anyone on the team?"

He looked at his fingernails. Somehow he felt she suspected. "Maybe." Then he looked at her. "Please give me another chance, Ms. Agard. I'll remember next time."

"You're sure?"

"Yes."

"Okay, Melvin. You may go."

"Thanks, Ms. Agard."

Of all his teachers he liked her the best. She seemed to understand him more than the others did. He was sorry he hadn't remembered the answer to her question, and somehow felt that he had let her down.

After school the Titans played their first league game. The Quincy Quints were their opponents. Caskie and Stoney started off in the forward positions, Mel and Rick Longfoot in the guard positions, and Skeet Robinson at center against Dutch Fullmer. Caskie scored the first basket from the corner, then Skeet laid one up and drew a foul at the same time.

The ball went in, so Skeet was allowed only one shot. He took his time at the foul line, shot the ball from his chest, and made it.

"Yea, Robinson!" shouted the Titan cheerleaders.

The Quints took out the ball, moved it cautiously downcourt. Across the center line they passed it quickly and carefully among themselves, the sound of the ball a whispering thump as it moved from one pair of hands to another.

Mel waited for a pass to be thrown to his man and saw it coming. He leaped in front of his opponent, grabbed the ball, and dribbled it hard upcourt. From the corner of his eye he saw a player, a player in a green uniform, running several feet to his left. Close behind him thundered another pair of running feet. But he was close to the basket now. He leaped and shot.

The ball brushed against the backboard, rolled around the rim, and dropped off!

"Yayeeeee!" screamed the Quints' fans.

"You . . . you . . . !" the boy in the green uniform glared at him. "Why didn't you pass it to me?" It was Caskie Bennett.

Mel said nothing. A Quint caught the rebound, dribbled it away from the basket, and passed to another Quint. Seconds later they scored.

At the end of the first quarter it was a 13–13 tie. Pedro Dorigez and Kim took Mel's and Skeet's places in the second period. By the end of the half there was still little change. It was 21–20 in favor of the Hillcrest Titans.

Darryl, in Stoney's place when the second half started, sank a corner shot. A minute later he scored three more points on a layup that drew a foul.

"Yea, Brady!" screamed the cheerleaders.

The Quints came back within a point of tying the score again. Titans' ball. Pedro Dorigez arced a pass to Mel. A Quint burst in, grabbed the pass, and dribbled downcourt for another two points that put them in the lead.

"Pedro!" snarled Caskie. But Pedro paid no attention to him.

The Titans caught up and by the fourth quarter they were leading 35–34. Mel caught a rebound, dribbled to the corner, and looked for someone to pass to. Stoney, back in the game, came running from the middle of the court, guarded closely by a

Quint. The Quints were playing a man-to-man defense, sticking so close to their men it seemed as if they were glued together.

Mel lobbed a pass to Stoney. Like a gold streak a Quint's arm reached out and intercepted the ball. The Quint dribbled in toward the basket, laid it up. In!

"Come on, will you?" Caskie snarled as he ran up close to Mel. "Look where you're throwing!"

Mel glared back at him and balled his fists. *Darn that Caskie!*

Darryl Brady pulled on his arm for an instant, grinned at him. "Come on, Mel. Let's play ball."

Mel relaxed his fists, took a deep breath, and ran down the court to cover his man.

A minute later Andy Head took Mel's place. "What went on out there, Mel?" asked Coach Tom Thorpe.

"Nothing," said Mel.

"Nothing?"

Mel shrugged. "It was nothing, Coach," he repeated.

The game ended with a squeaking win by the Titans, 48–47.

In the locker room Mel said to Darryl, "Let's get changed and take off."

"You're not going to shower?"

"No."

"Oh yes you are," said a new voice. Mel and Darryl looked up at Coach Thorpe who had just entered the room. "You're not leaving here without a shower. Neither one of you."

Mel and Darryl took their showers together. In the next shower stall Skeet Robinson smiled at them through the spray. Skeet Robinson. Tall and skinny as a baseball bat. A kid everybody liked and who liked everybody. There was only one in a million like Skeet.

A *lucky kid,* thought Mel.

3

Caskie wasn't in school the next afternoon. Somehow, Mel was glad. That afternoon he felt more at ease than he had felt in a long time.

Dad came home at six. Ordinarily he was happy and talkative, even though few dental patients went to him. They preferred Dr. Collins, whose office was next door in the same building. He was helping Dad get established.

Dad often joked when he came home, but today he was less cheerful and unusually quiet.

"Everything okay at the office, dear?" Mom asked.

"Mostly. But something happened that upset me a little," he admitted.

The table was set. The family was already sitting around it, waiting to eat.

"I'm starved," said Cindy. "Let's hurry up and eat!"

15

"Yeah, let's chow down!" said Robby.

"All right, now. Behave," said Mom, quietly but firmly.

They said their thanks to God and began eating. Mel wondered what had happened at the office. But he didn't question Dad, and neither did anyone else. Guess it was just for Mom's ear to hear.

Later that evening, Mel found his mother alone in the kitchen and asked her what had troubled Dad.

"Caskie's mother had an appointment for Caskie with Dr. Collins," she explained. "But Dr. Collins was called away on an emergency and his patients are being sent to Daddy. When Mrs. Bennett walked into Daddy's office and saw Daddy, she turned right around and went back out."

Mel asked, "Didn't they know Dad is a dentist?"

"I think they did. But perhaps Daddy's name, Dr. Jensen, didn't register until they saw him."

Anger gnawed at Mel as he walked to the kitchen door and looked out across the backyard and fence at the back of Caskie's place. The Robinsons lived next door to Mel. Their backyard joined the Bennetts' backyard. The lawns were practically burned to a crisp after a hot, dry summer.

"I don't know, Mom. I just don't know," he muttered, stuffing his hands hard into his pockets.

"About the Bennetts, you mean?"

"The Bennetts and anybody else who doesn't want us around."

"You heard what Dad said. They'll get used to us and we'll get used to them. They've got some wrong ideas about blacks because they've never known any. They just have to get to know us."

Mel plunked himself into a chair. "All the same, I'm glad I'm black," he said. "There's been a lot of famous African Americans, Mom. George Washington Carver, Booker T. Washington, and Jackie Robinson —" His eyes lit up. "He was the first black player in the major leagues! And there's Michael Jordan and Magic Johnson —"

"I know, I know," Mom interrupted, smiling. "Many more than you can count on those ten fingers of yours." Then she patted Mel's shoulder. "Don't fret about this. Everything will be all right — just wait and see."

Mom always seemed to make him feel a lot better.

4

The next day Ruth asked Mom if she could go skating with Connie Robinson that evening at the ice skating rink. Connie was Skeet's sister and they got along together as well as Mel and Skeet.

"Yes, you may go," Mom said. "But I don't think . . ."

"I wanna go too, Mommy!" interrupted Cindy. "Can I go, Mommy?"

"Me, too!" piped up Robby.

Mom smiled. It was always like that when one of them wanted to go somewhere for fun.

"Okay. You can all go," agreed Mom.

"Ruth, keep an eye on your sister. I'm not sure she can skate well enough yet without falling on her bottom a few times."

"I only fell *once* the last time, Mommy!" Cindy cried as if Mom were partially deaf.

"I bet!" laughed Mel.

Mel loved to skate. He never missed going to a skating party. Sometimes he wished it was winter all the time so that he could skate whenever he wanted to.

That afternoon the Titans played the yellow-uniformed Candor Bees in the Hillcrest school gym. Coach Thorpe put in the same starters as he had in the Quints game. Right off, Caskie sank a field goal from about twenty feet away, and Skeet a corner shot to put them into a 4–0 lead within the first thirty seconds.

One of the Bees took out the ball, dribbled across the center line, and then passed it cautiously among his teammates, waiting for an opportunity to shoot. Mel, who until now had covered his man like a hawk, suddenly found himself alone. The Bee had buzzed away from him. Before Mel realized what happened, the Bee passed the ball to another Bee. The Bee drove in and laid it up for two points.

"That was your man, Jensen!" shouted Caskie.

Mel tightened his lips, disgusted at himself and at the same time angry at Caskie. It seemed that Caskie enjoyed humiliating him every chance he had.

The basket was the spark the Bees needed to get going. They began sinking long ones from fifteen feet away . . . twenty. Once someone gave Mel a shove. He swung around, thinking it was a Bee. It was Caskie Bennett.

Seconds later Caskie was taken out and Pedro Dorigez was sent in to replace him. Mel saw the coach motion Caskie to sit beside him, saw him talk to Caskie. *Did he see Caskie shove me?* Mel thought. *Was that what he was asking Caskie about?* Mel wished he had extra hearing powers to really know.

Pedro took out the ball and passed to Mel. Mel dribbled it to the center line and passed to Rick. Rick feinted a shot at the basket, drawing his man out of the way, then drove in and tried a layup shot. The ball spun around the rim and rolled off.

Skeet, Mel, Rick, and a trio of Bees leaped for the rebound. Skeet got it, tried to pour it in. Again the ball rolled off the rim. The mad scramble for the ball continued. It bounced from fingertips to fingertips.

At last it landed on the floor and someone kicked it out of bounds.

Phreeeet! went the referee's whistle. "Yellow!" he shouted.

The Bees took out the ball, passing it down toward the Titans' basket. Again they very carefully passed it among themselves, trying to move the ball in close to the basket before shooting.

Seconds later Mel's man darted in front of him. Mel, alert, sprang to his side just as the pass was thrown. The Bee gave Mel a shove out of his way and caught the pass. The whistle shrilled and the referee pointed a finger at the Bee.

"Pushing!" He took the ball and handed it to a Titan, Pedro Dorigez.

Pedro took it out and passed to Skeet. Skeet passed to Mel. Mel drove in, saw a man in yellow sweep across his path, and leaped. Instead of shooting for the basket he snapped a pass to Skeet, who was running in from his left. Skeet caught the ball and rose with it. The ball rolled off his fingers and into the net.

The fans screamed.

"Nice shot, Skeet!"

"Nice play, Mel!"

But the quarter ended with the Bees leading 15–9. The same five Titans started the second quarter. Two minutes later Coach Thorpe sent in substitutes. Mel sat on the bench, breathing tiredly. He wiped the sweat off his forehead and face.

Caskie was in there now. Dribbling hard. Passing. There was no doubt that Caskie was good. But he didn't pass to Darryl. Several times Darryl was in the clear when Caskie or Stoney had the ball, but not once did either boy pass to him.

Aren't you going to say something to them, Coach? You must see what they're doing as well as I do.

The half ended with the Bees leading 29–21. Both teams trotted down to the locker room and rested. Mel relaxed on a bench next to a wall, his legs sprawled out in front of him, his eyes closed. Here it was so much cooler than up in that warm, crowded gym.

"I want you boys to know something right now," Coach Thorpe's strong voice cut into the silence. "There are five of you on that floor at the same time. Not three. Not four. But five! Pass when you have to. I don't care if it's to Rick, Skeet, Stoney, Mel, Darryl, or Caskie. You're all out there, playing on the same team. Make it a three-man team or a four-man team, and you'll see some changes made."

Coach Thorpe had seen what had been happening on the floor all right. He had seen every bit of it.

What the coach had said made some difference during the second half. But not much. Two or three times Caskie could have thrown a pass to Mel when Mel was in the corner, but Caskie didn't. He would either drive in for a basket himself or pass to one of the other players.

The score was closer at the end of the third period. In the fourth the Titans began sinking long ones that seemed to hit every time. Mel sank three, giving him a total of six field goals and one foul shot so far. Skeet had racked up about the same. But it was Caskie who led. When the game ended it was Titans 51–Bees 47.

The boys showered, and the late bus carried the Titans to their homes. That night Dad drove the young Jensens to the skating party.

The rink was crowded and noisy with the hum of excited skaters and blare of the loud music. Mel skated forward and backward, though he wasn't very good skating backward.

Whenever he passed by Ruth and Connie with Cindy between them, they would yell to each other and laugh. Once Mel took his brother Robby's hand and skated along with him. But after a trip around the floor they separated. Each preferred to skate by himself.

Snowflakes striking the windows of the double doors, leaving tearlike streaks as they melted, caught Mel's eyes. He stopped and saw fat flakes of snow whip across the tall light pole in the school parking lot, saw it changing the blacktop to white.

Few of the skaters paid any attention to the weather. They were too busy enjoying themselves to be bothered by what went on outside.

Suddenly the lights went out, throwing the room into a world of darkness. The music stopped. A girl screamed. And then another, and another. Someone bumped into Mel, knocking him against someone else. He fell and heard others fall.

The shouting continued — until a voice yelled out, "Quiet! Please be quiet!"

5

Mel rose to his feet. The cries subsided, until only the sound of skates was heard as their wearers tried to get to their feet and steady themselves.

"Please try to be as quiet as you can," pleaded the voice again. Mel recognized it now. It belonged to Mr. Thompson, the science teacher. "Try to get to the side of the rink and please take off your skates. You might run into someone and hurt him. If someone was hurt when the power went off, please be calm. We'll try to get light and take care of you then."

Mel saw that he was near the rear double glass doors of the rink. He skated to them, hopped off the ice to the floor, and removed his skates.

A hum started up among the crowd. Soon giggling

and laughter unwound the tension. Everyone was getting used to the darkness.

Glad Cindy is with Ruth and Connie, Mel thought. *She'd be crying her head off if she weren't.*

Minutes passed. Mel heard skates moving back and forth on the ice. The kids seemed to be getting restless. When were the lights coming back on? Was anybody doing anything about them?

Presently someone appeared from the hall with a flashlight. He swung the beam over the entire room. Nearly everybody was sitting down.

"What happened?" someone shouted.

"The lights went out!" another voice answered. A burst of laughter broke out.

"I mean what caused it, wise guy?"

"Don't know, yet," replied Mr. Thompson, the person with the flashlight. "Anyway, whatever it was caused the lights to go out all over town."

"You mean there are no lights at all in Trexton?" another voice piped up.

"That's right."

"Wow! We might have to stay here all night!"

"Cool!" shouted another gleefully.

Mel stood up and looked out through the window

of the door. The carpet of snow was getting thicker on the parking lot. The cars were beginning to look like strangely shaped blobs of white.

Mel accidentally leaned against the steel bar, pushing it down. The door jerked open, letting in a gust of wind and snow. Mel yanked it shut.

The minutes dragged. Mel got restless. He didn't like waiting in the darkness indefinitely for the power to come back on. He wasn't going to wait half the night, not with that snow coming down so thick and heavy.

But what about Ruth, Cindy, and Robby? He shouldn't leave without them. They'd worry about him if they didn't see him.

"Ruth!" he called out over the noise in the pitch darkness. "Ruth!"

He started after his coat, then paused. He would never find it. It was in the coatroom, hanging among a bunch of other coats. And the coatroom was behind that crowd of kids seated on the floor, hidden in the blackness of the huge room.

Glumly, he sat down, crossing his legs in scissor fashion. He'd have to wait just like the rest. There was nothing else to do.

Several students began singing. Others joined in, including Mel. Suddenly another flashlight beam appeared. It shifted around on the students, then focused on Mr. Thompson. The person holding the flashlight approached the teacher. The singing stopped. The rink hushed as the two persons had a brief conversation.

Then Mr. Thompson announced in a clear, loud voice, "It'll be another half hour before the power is restored. Please rest as comfortably as you can. As soon as the lights come on you can continue skating."

"Hooray!" someone shouted. Others took up the cry.

Half an hour later the lights came on. It seemed like an hour to Mel. The room was getting cold, and the cold was gnawing through Mel's clothing to his skin.

Everyone put their skates back on and started to skate again. The blades whispered on the ice. The music started to play. Smiles once again lit up the children's faces.

A boy, much smaller than Mel, lost his balance

and fell. Mel quickly switched direction and scooted for the boy. He heard someone skate up behind him as he reached the boy and lifted him to his feet.

"You okay?" Mel asked.

"Yes! Thanks!" The boy smiled at him and skated away.

Then Mel saw the skater behind him sweep by and look back. It was Stoney. Was Caskie Bennett here, too? Mel looked for him but didn't see him.

Skating time was extended for an extra half hour to make up for the time the power was off. Mel wanted to stay till the last minute, but Ruth insisted they had better go home. Robby and Cindy would have trouble getting up in the morning, and snow was piling up outside. They put on their coats and trudged through the snow that was already above their ankles.

They were almost home when a soft, tender cry broke the night's stillness.

"A kitten!" cried Ruth. "The poor little thing! Can you see it, Mel?"

The faint, ever-so-soft crying came from near a bush in front of a house. Mel plowed through the snow and saw what looked like a black and white ball almost buried there. He gathered it up and cuddled it against him.

"You nutty kitten," he said. "What are you doing out in this crazy weather?"

"Let me take him!" pleaded Cindy. "Please!"

"Not now. Wait'll we get inside," said Mel.

As soon as they entered the kitchen of their home where the light shone on them, Cindy exclaimed, "That kitten looks like Florie's! It is! It's Florie Bennett's!"

Mel's heart sank. Of all the people in Trexton, this kitten would have to belong to Caskie Bennett's sister.

6

Mel carried the kitten to the Bennetts' early the next morning. He was wondering what the Bennetts would say. Caskie met him at the door.

"Cindy said this kitten belongs to Florie," said Mel, holding up the kitten. 'We found it last night huddled in the snow near our house."

Caskie took the kitten. "Thanks," he said. "We were wondering where she was. Thanks a lot."

"We kept her in the house all night by the stove. Mom fed her milk, too."

"That's good," said Caskie. "I'll tell Florie. S'long."

"S'long," said Mel.

He was relieved and glad he had taken the kitten to the Bennetts' himself. And glad it was Caskie who had come to the door.

❀   ❀   ❀

On the basketball court, though, things hadn't changed a bit between Caskie and Mel. It was December 6 and the Titans were playing the Addison Comets. The Comets, wearing blue suits with crimson stripes, were as flashy as they looked. They led going into the second quarter by seven points.

"Toots Kinney's scoring most of the points, Coach," said Caskie Bennett irritably. "He's running circles around Mel."

Mel tried to hide his resentment. Toots was taller and a real fast man with the ball. But he wasn't running circles around anybody. He was taking long shots and making them.

"Those long sinkers are pretty hard to be stopped by anybody," said the coach. "We'll just have to make him hurry up his shots if he wants to keep taking those chances and hope that it shakes him up a little. Okay, Mel?"

Mel nodded. "Okay."

He guarded Toots Kinney closer in the second quarter, and Toots didn't take as many shots. The score at the end of the half read 28–21 on the electric scoreboard.

Pedro Dorigez started the second half in place of

Mel. He guarded the hot-handed Comet, but Toots Kinney was too fast for him. Twice in half a minute Toots feinted Pedro out of the way and drove in for layups. Then Andy Head, substituting for Stoney at right forward, passed to Pedro. Pedro threw to Caskie, only to see the ball intercepted and sunk for another two points. Almost everyone in the gym could hear Caskie's angry shout at Pedro.

"You crazy spic! Watch where you're throwing!"

The words were hardly out of Caskie's mouth when Pedro Dorigez rushed at him, both fists clenched, jaw squared. He swung at Caskie. Caskie took the blow on his right shoulder, staring at the enraged boy as if he couldn't believe his eyes. Caskie swung back, but Pedro's blows were nearly three to his one.

Phreeeeet! Phreeeeet! blasted the whistle. The referee rushed forward and Coach Thorpe jumped up from the bench.

"Stop it!" he yelled.

The boys stopped fighting and stood glaring at each other, Pedro much angrier and breathing harder than Caskie. Neither one said a word.

"You're both out of the game," said the referee.

Coach Thorpe took them both by their arms. "Sit down," he said disgustedly. "Caskie, I've warned you."

"I didn't say anything!" snarled Caskie.

"No, I guess not," said the coach. "Pedro sailed into you for saying nothing."

They reached the bench. "Darryl . . . Mel, get in there. Report to the scorekeeper."

Mel kept a hawklike watch on the Comets' star, Toots Kinney, keeping him down to six points. It was a tight game when it ended, the Titans squeezing out a 51–50 victory.

On Thursday the Titans played the Lansing Red Jackets. The Red Jackets wore red satin uniforms with white stripes, but their uniforms were much flashier than their performance on the court. Skeet scored on two hook shots in the first quarter and another in the second, besides his three layups and two foul shots, netting him fourteen points for the half. Mel had four field goals and a foul shot for nine.

The second half started with the Titans leading

39–19. Andy and Darryl went in at the forward positions, Pedro and Rick at guard, and Kim Nemeth at center. The Red Jackets' center, an inch taller than Kim, tapped the ball to a teammate who passed it quickly to another teammate running toward the sideline. A pass to the corner . . . an attempted shot . . .

Darryl jumped, blocked the shot, stole the ball, and started to dribble it upcourt. The ball struck his foot and skidded across the floor into an opponent's hands. The Red Jacket passed to a player at the right sideline. The player feinted Andy out of position, dribbled toward the basket, and leaped with the ball. A perfect layup.

Mel saw Darryl smacking his fist into a palm in disgust. It sure was tough luck.

Pedro took out the ball and passed to Darryl. Darryl bounced it to Kim, who dribbled across the center line, passed to Pedro, then raced across the keyhole. Pedro returned the pass to him and Kim laid it up for another two points. "Okay, Mel," said the coach. "Take Pedro's place."

Mel had the ball for only a moment before the

horn blew for the end of the third quarter. He played half of the final quarter, scoring two more field goals and a foul shot for a total of fourteen points, his best scoring so far. The Titans walked off with a 68–41 score.

Mel noticed one thing that had not happened in the last two games: in neither one had Stoney or Caskie yelled dirty remarks at him, Darryl, or Pedro. Was Coach Thorpe's warning paying off after all?

The game against the Putnam Crusaders was a different one altogether. The Crusaders, coming from the smallest school in the league, played as if they had been born and bred on the basketball court. Mel played the first quarter without scoring a point. He had two chances on fouls, but neither time did the ball cooperate for him.

Darryl did a little better. Two points better. A hook shot after a pass from Mel. The Putnam Crusaders, with their best man, Eddie Frish, heading the attack, led 29–20 at the end of the half.

Coach Thorpe put Mel on Eddie to slow up the hustling little player. Mel couldn't. The coach then put Caskie on him. Caskie slowed him up a little. Darryl tried it, too, but failed. Caskie seemed to be the best player to hold the purple-uniformed player down. But the entire Titan defense wasn't enough against the battling Crusaders, who won the game, 42–39.

A cold took hold of Mel on Wednesday night and kept him in bed all day Thursday. The Titans were playing the Beetles that afternoon and Robby stayed to see the game.

"We beat the Beetles," he said when he came home from school.

"What was the score?" asked Mel.

"Forty-eight to forty-one," answered Robby. "Caskie got nineteen points."

"I don't care what he got," grumbled Mel. "How many points did Skeet and Darryl get?"

"I don't know."

Mel didn't go to school on Friday either. His cold was better, but not much.

At ten-thirty, after the mail carrier had come, Mom brought in a letter to Mel. "Funny," she said. "It's got your name on it, but that's all. It doesn't even have a stamp."

Mel ripped open the envelope. The letter, dated

that day and addressed to him, was printed in pencil.

The Titans beat the Beetles 48 to 41. Why don't you stay home more often?

There was no signature.

7

After lunch Mel told his mother he felt much better and wanted to go outside for a few minutes. She was reluctant to let him at first, but finally agreed. He put on his boots, winter coat, and hat, and went out the back door.

The unstamped, unsigned letter he had received bothered him. He had a hunch who had put it in the mailbox. Only one person he knew would have the nerve to do a thing like that.

He stood on the porch awhile, the sun shining bright and warm against his face, touching high spots on the snow. He heard a door bang across the yard and saw Mrs. Bennett leaving the house. He watched her as she went to the garage and backed out the car.

Then he spotted the snowman in Caskie's yard.

He had seen Caskie and his sister Florie making it a couple of evenings ago, right after they had come home from school. It was a tall, fat snowman with extended arms and a dark hat on its large, round head. Mel guessed that it had eyes, nose, and a mouth, too, but he couldn't see them from where he was.

Looking at it reminded him of Caskie and the note, and anger smoldered again inside of him. He stepped down to the sidewalk Dad had shoveled clean, and trudged through the knee-high snow to the rear of the garage where he had a better view of the snowman.

He would tear it down, that's what he'd do. With Mrs. Bennett gone, no one was home. Mr. Bennett worked at a factory, and Caskie and Florie were in school.

Mel took a few more steps through the deep snow. Then he realized how foolish it was to walk through it to the Bennetts' backyard. Anybody could see instantly who had torn down the snowman if he continued to leave a trail through the backyard that way.

He walked down his driveway to the street and

around the block to the Bennetts' backyard. The snowman had eyes and a nose and a mouth all right. But he wasn't going to have them long. He wasn't even going to *be* there long.

Mel pulled out the two small red rubber balls that were the eyes and threw them aside. Then he yanked out the tin can that was the nose and the piece of three-inch-wide wood with teeth drawn on it and flung those aside. The snowman had no face at all now.

Mel stood peering at it. A horrible feeling suddenly came over him. He would regret this. He knew he would. Caskie would figure out easily that it was Mel who had torn down his snowman. There was no telling what Mr. and Mrs. Bennett would do then.

Mel picked up the rubber balls, the tin can, and the piece of wood and put them back on the snowman. Then he stood back and looked at it with satisfaction and returned home the same way he had come.

8

The next morning Mel and Darryl walked over to Pedro Dorigez's house where they found Pedro and Skeet Robinson playing with Pedro's small pool table in the basement. The cue balls were small and the cue sticks short. Mel had played with them before.

The boys spent an hour playing pool, then picked up their ice skates and walked a half mile to the river.

"Look! It's only frozen on the edges!" said Skeet disappointedly.

"Shoot," said Darryl. "Guess it just isn't cold enough to freeze over yet."

They headed back for their homes, carrying their skates over their shoulders.

"Who are we playing next week?" Mel asked. He

hadn't seen a basketball since Tuesday and he was getting anxious to play again.

"The Grafton Polaras," said Skeet. "I heard they've got a six-foot center. And he's only thirteen!"

"I know what we'll do," said Darryl grinning. "We'll put springs in your sneakers, Skeet!"

"Yeah!" said Skeet with a laugh.

The game, ending the first half of the season, was with the Polaras at the Grafton Middle School gym in Grafton, a town about sixteen miles from Trexton. The Titans left by bus at three o'clock, one bus carrying the players and cheerleaders, another carrying the spectators.

The Polaras, in orange uniforms with white stripes, started off with a three-point lead within fifteen seconds from the time the opening whistle blew. Herb Jones, their six-foot center, was fouled by Mel as he went up for a layup. The basket counted and he sank the foul shot.

"Hooray, Jones!" yelled the Polara cheerleaders and fans.

Mel saw Caskie shaking his head disgustedly. Stoney took out the ball, passed to Caskie. Caskie passed to Skeet. Rick curved around in front of Skeet, took Skeet's pass, dribbled to the corner. Guarded closely, he wasn't able to get off a shot. Then Stoney darted past his man and Rick bounced the ball to him. Stoney caught it, went up and pushed it against the boards. In!

"Yea, Stone! Yea, Stone!" yelled the Titan cheerleaders.

The Polaras chalked up another layup by Herb Jones, then a set by a fast little towhead. Mel tried a set when he got the ball, missed, rushed in for the rebound, got it, tried to tip it in. Failed.

A scramble followed. Mel got the ball. A Polara tried to take it from him. Jump ball.

Mel tapped it to Skeet. Skeet dribbled in close, was blocked by a guard, leaped, passed to Rick. Rick passed to Mel going in toward the basket from the corner. Mel caught it high, jumped, sank it.

"Yea, Jensen!"

The Polaras sank a couple more. Rick dumped a twenty-footer. At the end of the first quarter it was Polaras 11–Titans 6.

The Polaras were just as strong during the second

quarter. They sank one from the corner, another from the keyhole. A layup by Jones.

Caskie, running constantly, kept chattering at his Titan teammates. "C'mon! Let's go! Let's stop 'em! Rick, get in there! Don't let 'em pass! Skeet, keep moving! Mel, guard your man! You're slowing down!"

Caskie seemed to have more energy than three guys put together.

He sank a long one, drove in for a layup, made the basket, and was fouled. The crowd screamed. The sounds died away. The crowd waited, silently. Caskie bounced the ball, shot. In!

Andy Head went in, Stoney out. Darryl went in. Caskie out. But not for long. Caskie was back in with two minutes to go in the first half. In those two minutes he scored four points. Pedro, in for Mel, was fouled and scored his shot. Both teams had found the basket and were plunking them in. The score at halftime: Polaras 29–Titans 27.

The Titans struggled hard through the third quarter, but something was different this time. Their long shots were not hitting, as if something had been taken away from both teams during halftime.

Then Caskie exploded, sinking two layups, one after another. The Titans tied the score. They went into the lead. They began stretching the margin wider and wider. A five-point lead . . . then seven points . . .

It was Polaras 44–Titans 51 at the end of the third quarter.

"Let's keep it up!" said Coach Thorpe as he stood among his Titan players during the one-minute rest period. "You guys are doing great! Every one of you."

The Polaras had the ball at the start of the fourth period. They took it out, passed it to their front court, passed it carefully. Mel guarded his man closely, sticking to him as if he were magnetized.

Suddenly the man bolted away, took a quick pass from the tall center, and drove in for a layup. It was good.

"Your man, Mel!" shouted Caskie.

Thanks, thought Mel. *As if I didn't know.*

Rick took out the ball, passing it to Mel. Mel bounced it to Stoney. . . . It was intercepted! The Polara dribbled it all the way downcourt and sank it!

"You dope!" Caskie shouted. "Watch where you're passing!"

That was it. Mel could take no more. He charged after Caskie. The whistle shrieked. The referee caught Mel's arm. A horn honked loudly. Kim went in, motioning Caskie out.

"Caskie," said Coach Thorpe angrily, "I warned you! You're benched indefinitely!"

9

Mel tried not to glance over at Caskie sitting on the bench. But after Rick passed Mel the ball from out of bounds and he passed it on to Kim, he looked. Caskie had his elbows on his knees and his head bowed.

Benched indefinitely, the coach had said. How long was indefinitely? How good were the Titans with Caskie out of the game?

Mel turned his attention back to the game. Kim was dribbling the ball upcourt. Across the center line he paused, holding the big orange sphere in his hands. A Polara swung around in front of him, struck the ball, and knocked it out of his hands. Kim retrieved it, dribbled toward the basket, and shot. The ball struck the backboard, then the rim, and bounced off.

Kim, Mel, and a couple of Polaras leaped for the rebound. Mel struggled through the white, sweating bodies as if everything depended on his getting possession of the ball. He, the whole team, had to play harder now that Caskie was out of the game.

Then he had the ball, gripping it tightly in both hands, shoving his elbows back and forth like pistons to throw off the Polaras. He dribbled low and fast toward the corner. His guard followed him, waving long arms like a fast-flying bird. Skeet ran up behind the guard, and Mel bounced a pass to him under the guard's left arm. Skeet caught the ball, spun, leaped, tossed for the basket. In!

Mel cast a quick glance at the scoreboard. VISITORS — 48; HOME — 53. *How much time was left?* he wondered anxiously.

Polaras' ball. They took it out, moved it hastily downcourt, passed it back and forth in a half circle just beyond the center line. Mel kept a tight guard on his man. The Titans had a five-point lead. They had to keep it. They had to, or Caskie would say that the Titans could do nothing without him.

A Polara broke fast toward the basket. A pass

zipped like an orange streak to him. He caught it, leaped. A layup!

"Mel! Rick! Get down here!" shouted Coach Thorpe.

Mel and Rick ran hard to their front court. Kim passed to Skeet. Skeet whipped it to Rick. Rick broke for the basket, shot, missed. The Polaras' center caught the rebound, passed to a teammate. In hardly any time at all the ball was at the opposite end of the court, a Polara leaping up with the ball. Another layup! Titans 53–Polaras 52.

Mel, sweat dripping down his face, glanced at the clock. A minute and eleven seconds to go!

He saw Coach Thorpe standing up, motioning for time-out. "Time!" Mel shouted to the referee.

"Time!" echoed the ref. He took the ball and held it under his arm while he stood in the out-of-bounds area at one side of the basket.

"Slow down," said Coach Thorpe. "You're getting all shook up out there. Get the ball, hang on to it as much as you can. Work close to the basket. Don't shoot until you're almost sure of making it."

Mel wiped the sweat off his face and forehead with a towel, passed it to the next guy. Then he looked at Caskie sitting alone on the bench, staring at the floor with a sad, faraway expression on his face and in his eyes. Mel wondered about him a moment, then looked at the coach. "Coach," he said, "would — would you please put Caskie back in the game? We need him to win."

The coach and the other Titans stared at Mel. "Sorry, but I'm not going back on my word."

The coach kept looking at Mel as if mulling over what Mel had said to him.

And then time was up. The boys returned to the court.

I wish he had put Caskie back in, thought Mel. *I really wish he had.*

It was the Titans' ball. Rick took it out, passed to Skeet. Skeet worked it cautiously upcourt. His guard went after him like a hornet and forced him to pass. Rick caught it, whipped it to Mel who was skirting around behind him. Mel dribbled down the sideline, stopped as his guard began windmilling his arms again, and bounce-passed to Skeet. Skeet dribbled up to the basket and then, like a small bolt of lightning, a Polara stole the ball from Skeet and dribbled away downcourt!

He passed to another Polara running near the left sideline. The Polara caught it, stopped near the corner, took a set. A basket! The Polaras went into the lead, 54–53.

Mel looked at the clock. Thirty-two seconds to go!

Again Rick took out the ball, passed to Mel. Mel passed to Skeet, then glanced at the bench. Caskie had his head up now. He was watching the game, looking sad as ever.

Skeet dribbled upcourt, started to break fast for the basket when a Polara rushed at him from the side and struck at the ball. Whack! His hand struck Skeet's instead. The whistle shrilled.

"One shot!" yelled the ref.

"C'mon, Skeet! Make it!" cried the Titan fans.

Skeet stood at the foul line, accepted the ball from the ref, bounced it once . . . twice . . . then poised himself and shot.

The crowd seemed to hold its breath. The ball struck the backboard, then the rim, and bounded off!

Skeet, Mel, Rick, they all — including the Polaras — rushed in for the rebound. Mel got it, leaped, missed the shot!

"Eight! . . . Seven! . . . Six! . . . Five! . . . Four! . . ." The fans counted off the remaining seconds of the game.

Skeet got the ball, shot. Missed again! "Three! . . . Two! . . . One!"

The horn buzzed. It was over. The Polaras had won.

"We should've won it," said Darryl glumly as he walked down the steps to the locker room with Mel. "The guys choked."

"We should've," agreed Mel. "We would've, too, if Caskie had been playing."

He was sorry he had lost his temper. Sorry he had charged after Caskie.

But will Caskie ever get over his feelings about me? What can I do to make us friends?

Wednesday morning, just after Mel's third period ended and he was walking to his next class, he saw a person in the hall, a familiar person.

Mrs. Bennett could be here for only one reason.

10

That afternoon Mel met Coach Thorpe in the hall. The coach merely greeted him with a casual, "Hi, Mel," smiled, and went on by him without saying anything more.

Had Mrs. Bennett really been here to see the coach? Had they come to a showdown? Did she scare him into putting Caskie back into the next game? Mel wondered if he would learn the answers to those questions before Thursday's game.

That evening the Trexton Journal carried the summaries of the Titans-Polaras game.

TITANS (53)				POLARAS (54)		
	G	F	T		G	F	T
Bennett	8	1	17	Banfield	5	2	12
Stone	2	2	6	Kroller	4	1	9
Robinson	4	2	10	Jones	9	3	21
Jensen	4	1	9	Bishop	3	1	7
Longfoot	1	0	2	Shafer	0	0	0
Head	0	1	1	Battista	1	1	3
Dorigez	1	1	3	McNolen	1	0	2
Nemeth	0	1	1				
Brady	2	0	4				
Totals	22	9	53	Totals	23	8	54

On Thursday afternoon the Titans played the Quints in the Titans' gym, and Caskie Bennett wasn't there. Apparently Coach Thorpe had won the discussion he had had with Mrs. Bennett — if the reason for her visit at the school was the coach's benching her son.

It was a good thing the Quints were not a hot team, thought Mel. They had lost all their seven games the first half of the season, putting them at the very bottom of the league. Mel and the other members of the Titans were quite sure the Quints would give them very little trouble.

Andy Head started at the left forward position in place of Caskie. He did a lot of running and tried to be in the midst of the action as often as possible. Andy was working hard to make himself worthy of the position.

But Andy lacked something that made Caskie the excellent player he was. He couldn't dribble half as well as Caskie. Nor could he shoot baskets like Caskie. Caskie was a natural athlete. There were few guys in the league, thought Mel, who could out-play him. He hated to admit it because of the way Caskie behaved toward him. But Caskie was good. Real good for his age and size.

Andy sank a long set shot. Then a Quint struck his arm as he shot another time; Andy dumped in both foul shots. Mel scored a layup, then a crazy hook shot which he could hardly believe. He had taken a pass from Skeet, dribbled past the basket, then had leaped and shot the ball over his left shoulder, giving it a spin with his hands. The ball sank through the hoop without touching it.

In the second quarter Coach Thorpe put in Pedro Dorigez and Darryl in place of Mel and Andy. In the very first play Pedro fouled a Quint as the Quint tried a set. It was a two-shot foul, and Mel almost expected to hear a shout from Caskie. But Caskie wasn't there.

The Quints ran and played recklessly and were careless with their throws. Now and then their coach yelled at them, but it did very little good. The poor Quints just could not play well. They trailed at the half, 31–16.

They were all afire at the start of the second half. Their center, Dutch Fullmer, sank a twenty-footer, then got fouled on a layup that went in. He scored the foul shot and the Quints' fans went wild. But the Titans scored almost two points to their one.

Skeet sat out most of the fourth quarter after scoring nineteen points. Coach Thorpe didn't believe in giving any weak opponent a severe beating, so he let his reserves finish the game.

The Titans took it, 58–47.

It snowed on Christmas Eve. Some of the neighbors joined in a carol-singing group. They stopped in front of the Jensen house and sang "It Came Upon a Midnight Clear" and "The First Noel."

All the Jensens stood beside the brightly decorated Christmas tree in the living room and watched the singers through the wide picture window. As the group finished singing, one of them — Mrs. Hull, a neighbor a few doors away — motioned for the Jensen children to come out and join them.

"Can we, Mom?" asked Ruth, her eyes shining brightly. "It'll be fun!"

"Okay," said Mom.

Ruth, Mel, Robby, and Cindy put on their coats and boots and ran out to join the carolers, who were already singing in front of the next house.

They went around the block, singing in front of each house. At last they came to the Bennett house. Behind a window Mel could see part of their Christmas tree blazing with bright bulbs, tinsel, and colored lights that blinked off and on.

The carolers began singing. Soon Florie Bennett, and then Mrs. Bennett, both smiling, came to the window and watched them. All at once Mrs. Bennett's eyes encountered Mel and the other Jensen children. Her smile faded a little, then brightened again.

A face pressed forward between them. And then another. It was Caskie and his father. They smiled at the carolers. Mel and his brother and sisters were in back of the group. Mel saw the Bennetts look directly at them. The Bennett family stood there, watching, listening, smiling. When the carolers were finished and began walking toward the next house, the Bennetts waved to them.

It turned out to be a very joyful, merry Christmas Eve.

11

The next Titan game was against the Candor Bees on Tuesday, January 3, the same day school started. How fast vacation had gone! Mel had wished it could last and last, but vacations never do. He knew that.

The Bees, who had won only two games so far during the season, started buzzing almost the instant they got on the floor. Their yellow uniforms looked bright and clean as if they all had been laundered over the vacation.

Mel saw that Caskie was in the starting lineup today, and was glad. He had practically forgotten Caskie's calling him a "dope" and other names.

The Bees' frisky left forward, a yellow-haired boy with a face full of freckles, pumped in two baskets within the first two minutes. Skeet dropped one in from the side, then assisted Mel with a basket when he tossed a quick pass to Mel tearing in from the keyhole. Mel's layup almost didn't go in. The ball circled around the rim a couple of times before dropping through the net.

The Bees' Number 15, a tall, dark-haired boy with glasses, sank a long one. The freckle-faced boy dropped one in from the side. They were hitting them, Mel saw, from nearly all directions. It didn't seem possible that this could be the same team that had finished next to the cellar the first half of the playing season. At the end of the first period it was Bees 16–Titans 8.

Caskie opened up in the second quarter. He dumped in a set from the corner, then sank a layup which drew a foul when a Bee ran into him.

Caskie missed the foul shot. A wild scramble resulted under the basket, with the ball finally scooting across the floor toward the crowd. Darryl bolted after it. But the ball rolled into the crowd before he could reach it, and the referee yelled, "Yellow!"

The Bees took out the ball, moved it to their end

of the court, then lost it on a fumble. Rick retrieved the ball and shot to Skeet, who dribbled it back up-court. Across the center line he passed to Mel. Mel faked a throw to Darryl, then ran in toward the basket, his guard racing at his side like a shadow. Mel stopped on a dime and the guard glided by. Before he could get back to Mel, Mel set himself and took a shot. In!

The Bees took out the ball but lost it again. This time it was on an interception by Darryl, who broke away fast, dribbled all the way upcourt, and laid it up for two points. Darryl came away from the stage, which he had bumped up against, his dark face creased in a broad smile.

"Boy! Once I move, I *move!*" he said, loud enough for the crowd to hear. They laughed heartily. Darryl always drew a laugh.

At the end of the half the score was tied.

Something seemed to have happened to the Bees after halftime was over. The spark they had had at the beginning of the game seemed to have been smothered. They couldn't sink their shots. Now and then a Bee was called on a traveling violation. Their passes were intercepted. They trailed at the close of the third period by fifteen points. When the game was over the Titans were winners, 71–50.

Riding home on the bus Mel and Skeet sat behind Caskie and Stoney. Caskie turned around. "How many points, Mel?"

"Eleven," said Mel.

Caskie grinned. "Beat you by two," he said. "I got thirteen."

On Thursday the Titans romped over the Comets, 41–30. The next Tuesday they gave the Red Jackets a lacing, 49–40. They were on a hot winning streak, it seemed. On Thursday afternoon, January 12, the Crusaders from Putnam came over and started off the first quarter as if they owned the court. They had hustle, noise, and an accurate eye for the basket.

"Someone gave those boys a shot in the arm with some good medicine, Coach," remarked Darryl after Caskie called for a time-out. "They're hittin' from all over."

"I see," said Coach Thorpe. "Let's press them. Each man cover his man closely. Just make sure you don't foul."

The full-court press helped the Titans. It slowed

down the Crusaders. But when the first quarter was over the Crusaders were leading 11–5.

Pedro Dorigez scored the first basket in the second period from the keyhole spot. Darryl dumped in a layup and came away grinning and drawing a laugh from the crowd. Then the Crusaders rallied, picking up two baskets in a hurry and a foul on Caskie Bennett.

The Crusader sank the foul shot. Again Pedro scored from the keyhole spot. Mel, watching from the bench while Pedro was in for him, clapped happily. *Just hope he doesn't play so well that the coach won't put me back in!* he thought.

But Mel played the full final quarter, dumping in two baskets. Darryl, who was playing his best tonight, sank another just as the final whistle blew. It was Titans 48–Crusaders 40.

Mel and the rest of the team rushed into a huddle with their coach. "'Ray, Crusaders!" they yelled, then ran over to the Crusaders, shook hands quickly, and headed for the showers.

"Do you know," said Darryl as he stripped off his uniform in the locker room, "there are only two more games to play, and then the season's all over? And if we win those two we'll have a perfect record this second half?"

"No, I didn't know," said Mel. "I hadn't kept that close track."

"Well, you know now," said Darryl, and giggled that crazy giggle of his.

The next Saturday morning was really cold. Mel, Darryl, and Skeet draped their ice skates over their shoulders and walked the six blocks to the river. It was frozen all the way across and as far up and down as Mel could see.

"Guess some people get up before we do," observed Darryl. There were a dozen boys and girls on the ice, skating close to shore. Mel recognized Caskie Bennett, his sister Florie, Stoney, and some other kids who went to their school.

"Hope it's solid," said Mel.

"Why? Want to skate across?" asked Skeet.

"I was thinking about it."

"Doesn't look too good out toward the middle," said Skeet. "Looks like cracks out there."

"Well, come on," urged Mel. "Let's get our ice skates on."

They slid down the bank on the hard crust of snow, sat on the long, dried log on the shore, took off their shoes, and put on their skates.

"Let's race down to that rock and back!" said Darryl.

The three boys sped down the smooth surface of ice to a boulder that projected like an iceberg some one hundred yards away. Darryl led for a while, with Skeet and Mel close behind. Then Mel pressed ahead of Darryl. Within twenty feet of the boulder Skeet broke into the lead, circled around the boulder, then dashed back up the ice. Skeet won by at least twenty feet, with Mel a close second and Darryl trailing.

"Look," said Skeet. "Stoney and Caskie are going to skate across."

"Let's follow 'em," said Darryl and broke into a fast sprint after the two boys. Mel started after him, and then Skeet.

"Hey!" someone shouted. It sounded like Stoney. "The ice is cracking!"

Caskie, trailing Stoney by about ten feet, circled around and turned back toward shore. Then Stoney slowed up and turned, too. Just as he took a stride the ice gave away under him.

"Hey!" he shouted. He flung up his hands to catch an edge of the ice, but what he clutched broke in his hand. Down he went.

12

Caskie skated in a half circle, then headed toward the opened place in the ice where Stoney had fallen in. Mel, a few feet farther away, sped for the broken spot, too.

"Careful!" someone shouted from shore. "Don't get too close to that hole!"

Mel darted a glance over his shoulder and saw two of the older boys coming toward them. Six or seven feet from the hole Mel and Caskie pulled up, ice spraying from the sharp blades of their skates.

"Stoney!" yelled Caskie, crouching over. "Stoney!"

"He's gone!" Mel shouted, panic taking hold of him. Something inside him seemed to break into pieces. No matter what Stoney had said to him in the past, no matter how he had acted toward Mel on the basketball court, all that was forgotten now. Suddenly he saw a hand rise above the water near the edge of the ice. And then Stoney's head bobbed up!

"Stoney!" Mel and Caskie shouted in one voice.

Stoney spat out a mouthful of water and gulped in air. He brushed away his hair that had matted over his eyes and reached his hands out toward the boys.

Mel felt hands grip his ankles. He looked back and saw one of the older boys crouched behind him. Another older boy was getting into the same position behind Caskie, gripping his ankles too.

"Grab his hands and lift at the same time!" one of the boys ordered Mel and Caskie. "We'll pull you back on the ice!"

Mel and Caskie grabbed Stoney's hands and the bigger boys behind them pulled. Gradually they had Stoney safely out of the water and onto solid ice. He was breathing hard and seemed too tired to rise to his feet.

The older boys and Mel and Caskie rose and helped Stoney up. "Come on, Stoney. We'll drive you to the hospital."

Stoney wiped water off his face. His lips were purple and trembling. "I — I'm freezing," he chattered.

The two bigger boys, who Mel guessed were in

their late teens, took Stoney's arms. "Come on. We'll take you in my car," one of them said.

Mel and Caskie looked at each other. "Maybe you'd better tell Stoney's folks," suggested Mel.

"Yeah. Guess I better." Caskie brushed ice and water off his clothes and sprinted toward shore, flecks of ice leaping from his skates. Skeet and Darryl skated up beside Mel.

"You okay, Mel?" asked Darryl.

"I'm okay."

"Want to keep skating or you want to go home?" asked Skeet.

Mel didn't reply immediately. He was thinking. "We ought to put up a sign before somebody else breaks through the ice," he said.

"I've got some boards and paint at home," said Skeet. "I'll make one and put it up."

"How are you going to stand up a sign on this ice?" Darryl questioned.

"Easy. I'll nail the sign on a post and stick the post into a pail of dirt."

"You're a smart boy, Skeet," Mel said, smiling. "Let's get going."

Mel saw Stoney in the hall of the school on Monday.

"Hi, Stoney," he greeted, not sure whether Stoney would stop to speak to him or not. "How long were you in the hospital?"

But Stoney stopped. He even smiled a little. "Just a couple of hours. Thanks for helping me out of the water."

"That's okay," said Mel. "Glad you're all right." He waved and went on.

In the classroom he met Caskie face to face. "Hi, Caskie."

"Hi," answered Caskie. "I heard you and Skeet put that sign on the ice."

"No. Just Skeet," replied Mel.

"Well, anyway." Caskie picked up a book, notebook, and ballpoint pen from his desk. "But someone should've put one up before." He started past Mel. "See you."

"See you," echoed Mel.

The news of the rescue was in the local newspaper with a warning for skaters to be aware of thin ice on the frozen river. It was the first time that Mel had had his name in the paper for anything other than sports. He cut the clipping out and pasted it in his scrapbook.

The Titans played the Sun City Beetles on Tuesday afternoon, and the rescue of Stoney seemed practically forgotten.

The Titans had a perfect record so far this second half. The Beetles were a close second, with two losses out of five games. It should be a tight game. And a good one, if we win, thought Mel hopefully.

Tom White, the Sun City Beetles' tall, skinny right forward, grabbed the tap from center, dribbled around the keyhole to the corner, and took a set. A perfect shot!

Rick took out the ball, passed to Skeet, and Skeet

carelessly passed to Caskie. A black-uniformed player swept in like a bat, intercepted the ball, and passed it to another Beetle. The Beetle sank it. It was Tom White, the skinny forward.

"Skeet!" yelled Caskie. "Watch your passes!"

Rick took it out again. This time the Titans were more careful of their throws. They moved the ball down cautiously across the center line. Caskie caught a pass from Stoney, started to break fast for the basket, then stopped abruptly as a guard sprang in front of him. Mel trotted toward the corner, ready for but not expecting a pass from Caskie.

Then Caskie passed — directly to Mel! Mel caught the ball, drove in under the basket, leaped. A layup!

In quick, short passes the Beetles moved the ball to their front court. A small, stout-legged boy took a set from the foul line and sank it. Rick took out the ball and passed to Skeet. Skeet passed to Stoney. Stoney dribbled across the center line where a Beetle rushed at him, forcing Stoney to pass wildly. The ball sailed into the stands where one of the fans caught it.

"Black's ball!" shouted the ref.

A Beetle took it out. Mel flashed forward, stopped

the ball with his right hand, and dribbled it upcourt. Down the sideline opposite him was Caskie, running as hard as he could. A Beetle came up alongside Mel, and Mel passed over his head to Caskie. Caskie caught the ball, dribbled twice toward the basket, and shot. Two points!

Caskie ran up behind Mel. "Nice pass, Mel."

Mel looked at him and grinned. "Thanks, Caskie."

The Titans evened the score a few moments later. Beetles' out. They brought the ball downcourt, bounce-passed to Tom White. White leaped for a layup, missed. Skeet, Mel, and two Beetles jumped for the rebound. Mel got it, raced back upcourt, leaped. The ball rippled through the net just as a hand struck his.

"One shot!" yelled the ref. "Basket counts!"

Voices called out to Mel. "Come on, Mel! Come on, kid! Make it!" Among them Mel recognized Stoney's voice.

Mel went to the free-throw line, took the ball from the referee, and measured the basket. Carefully, he shot.

The ball struck the backboard, rolled around the rim, and then off.

14

A sea of arms. A clash of shoulders. A loud thump as a Titan fell on the floor. And then Skeet had the rebound. He dribbled it away from under the basket and passed to Stoney. Stoney took a set. It hit! The horn blew at the same time, ending the first quarter.

"You're moving like clockwork." Coach Thorpe was smiling proudly. "Skeet, you and Darryl keep close watch on Tom White. He's quick and accurate with his shots."

"We'll stop him, Coach," Darryl promised, wiping his sweating face with a towel.

Mel looked for Caskie and saw him kneeling, tightening the laces of his sneakers. When Caskie rose Mel looked away, then back again. But Caskie's attention was directed at the coach.

The starting team led off in the second period. A

minute later Coach Tom Thorpe sent in substitutes. Pedro Dorigez missed a twenty-footer, then ran up to the basket, leaped, caught the rebound, leaped again and sank it. A howl burst from the Titan fans.

"Yea, Dorigez!" yelled the cheerleaders.

The Beetles put on a scoring spree, picking up six points.

Then Darryl Brady intercepted a pass from a Beetle and heaved a long throw across the floor to Skeet. Skeet was tall but not tall enough. Darryl's pass sailed over his head into the crowd. Later Darryl sank a set shot to redeem himself, and then a foul shot. The first half ended with the Titans leading by three points.

In the third quarter the Beetles came back strong and crept ahead of the Titans. They held their lead going into the final period. Caskie had the ball, dribbling it in the corner with his man guarding him closely. Mel trotted up behind the man and Caskie bounced the ball skillfully to him.

"Sink it, Mel!" he said.

Mel caught the pass, spun, and leaped at the same time. The ball cleared the rim perfectly.

The score on the electric scoreboard read 46–41,

Beetles' favor, and there were five minutes left to play. The Beetles took out the ball and moved it across the center line, care taken with each pass to prevent an interception. The Titans kept up a tight press, hugging their men as closely as possible without risking a foul.

But then it happened. Mel's man caught a high pass, turned quickly, and bumped into Mel. *Phreeet!* went the referee's whistle, and up went a finger. Mel's shoulders collapsed. The Beetle strode to the free-throw line, accepted the ball from the ref, bounced it twice, then shot. In. 47–41.

Mel glanced at Caskie, expecting an icy stare. But Caskie wasn't looking at him. Caskie was running toward the corner, his attention on Stoney who was taking out the ball. A Beetle kept jumping in front of Stoney, arms waving up and down like wings to stop Stoney's pass in. Stoney bounced the ball under his right arm to Caskie and Caskie dribbled it upcourt.

Two men stopped him and Caskie passed. The ball was a perfect throw to Mel as Mel ran across the keyhole toward the basket. He caught it and, without changing his speed, went up with the ball. A basket!

The crowd exploded with a yell.

The Titans' close press kept the Beetles from advancing too near the basket. And the Beetles didn't dare to take a long shot for fear of missing and losing the ball to the Titans.

The Beetles kept throwing short passes and dribbling. Now and then the Beetle in possession of the ball would glance at the clock, and Mel knew he was just waiting for the seconds to tick by. The less time there was for the Titans to dump in baskets, the better. Mel knew it was up to the Titans to get the ball as often as they possibly could.

Then, suddenly, a Beetle drove in under the basket and shot. The ball struck the hoop, bounded off, and a field of hands went up for the rebound. Mel grabbed it, pulled it out of a Beetle's hands, and passed to Kim who dribbled the ball upcourt. Now it was the Beetles who put a tight press on the Titans. Kim tried to bouncepass the ball to Pedro Dorigez, but the ball struck his guard's knee and glanced off toward the keyhole. Mel scooped it up, leaped to shoot, and saw Caskie running in from the corner. He passed to Caskie and Caskie laid it up neatly against the boards. A basket!

Caskie smiled at Mel as they ran back to cover their men. The Titans continued to play well defensively, but were unable to score enough to overtake the Beetles. The score was 49–46 when the game ended.

15

In the locker room, just before the Titans-Polaras game, Coach Thorpe said, "Let's win this game, boys. It's our last and it will give us a good year — the most wins in the league. But win or lose we have a treat in store for us. A spaghetti dinner at Mama Torelli's! How about that?"

"All right!" the boys shouted.

"Do I love spaghetti!" Mel cried.

"With lots of sauce!" said Caskie, rubbing his stomach.

Five minutes after the game had begun the Titans realized that the Polaras were no pushover. They had lost only four games during the entire season and apparently they were in no mood to drop another.

Once in the first quarter Mel fouled a Polara and committed another foul in the second. Both times the Polara player scored his shot. Mel almost expected Stoney or Caskie to explode with some remark to him, but neither did. Matter of fact, he could hardly remember the last time when either one had yelled a nasty remark at him.

He passed to Caskie a couple of times when he was close enough to the basket to shoot at it himself, but both times Caskie was in a better position to shoot and both times he hit. They were playing well together.

When did Caskie really change his feelings toward me? wondered Mel. He realized then that Caskie hadn't changed all at once, but a little at a time. It had happened so gradually that Mel had hardly noticed the change. And, apparently, neither had Caskie. But now, thinking back, Mel noticed the change all right.

At the half the Polaras led, 31–25.

"Let's get them this second half," urged Caskie, plunking himself down beside Mel in the locker room.

Darryl looked at them and a broad smile came over his face. "You guys don't think you're going to do it alone, do you? The rest of us are going to do it, too."

In the third quarter Mel took advantage of every situation that came up, shooting when he had a good opportunity, passing when he didn't.

He sank three baskets and a foul shot for seven points. Caskie sank four. Stoney and Darryl scored six points between them. But the Polaras scored eight baskets, sixteen points, to put them in the lead by one point at the end of the third period, 47–46.

The Polaras struggled hard to keep their lead in the fourth and final period. Darryl Brady sent the fans into hysterics when he jumped as high as he could and hooked a shot that circled the rim twice before it dropped through the laces. Skeet sank a twenty-footer, then dropped in two successive foul shots that put the Titans ahead of the Polaras, who had sunk only two baskets so far.

With a minute to go the Polaras, fighting hard, scored a long one that put them ahead, 53–52. The Titan cheerleaders started a loud, armswinging cheer:

One! Two! Three! Four!
Who are we for?
Titans! TITANS! TITANS!

Thirty seconds to go. Mel took a shot from the corner. It missed! Skeet went up for the rebound, and came down with both his hands and a Polara's hanging desperately onto the ball.

"Jump!" yelled the ref.

Skeet tapped the ball. Caskie got it, dribbled back, passed to Mel in the corner. Mel took a set. In! 54–53!

The Polaras took out the ball. Herb Jones fumbled it and Caskie recovered it. Mel glanced at the clock. Fifteen seconds to go!

"Let's hang on to the ball, Caskie!" Mel shouted.

Caskie grinned and tossed the ball back to him. Mel passed to Stoney, Stoney to Skeet, Skeet to Darryl as the Polaras jumped back and forth, trying hard to grab the ball.

They couldn't. The horn buzzed, long and loudly. The game was over. The Titans had won, 54–53.

The boys jumped up and down and flung their

arms around each other. Their cheers were almost drowned out by the yelling from the Titan fans.

"Can you believe it!" cried Mel.

"We said we'd do it, didn't we?" said Caskie, sweat glistening on his smiling face.

"Sure did!" chuckled Darryl.

They ran to the Polara players and shook hands. The poor Polaras sure looked unhappy over their defeat. Then the Titans returned to the middle of the floor where Coach Thorpe greeted them with a handshake for each one.

"Nice going, boys. Ready for that spaghetti dinner?"

"And how!" said Mel. "I'm starved!"

"So am I!" said Caskie, strolling off the floor with Mel and Stoney. "Let's get showered and go!"